Postman Pat® and the
Magic Lamp

SIMON AND SCHUSTER

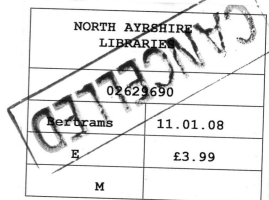

It was a busy day in Greendale. Ted Glen was painting the shed when Pat arrived on his rounds. "Careful, Pat," laughed Ted, "you don't want a red uniform!"

At Greendale farm, Charlie was showing Tom his new scientific calculator, and Katy was practising her skateboard moves!

"My turn now!" said Tom.

Tom wobbled off on the skateboard.

"Careful!" cried Katy.

Too late – Tom crashed into a pile of junk!

"It's no good, I can't do it," he sighed.

But Tom soon cheered up when he spotted an old lamp amongst all the rubbish.

"Hey, look at this," he said, rubbing the dirt off.

"Mind the genie doesn't come out!" chuckled Katy.

"Yeah! You'll get three wishes, like in Aladdin!" joked Charlie.

"Really?" said Tom. "Well, I wish I could ride a skateboard!"

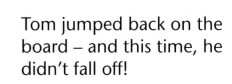

Tom jumped back on the
board – and this time, he
didn't fall off!

"I did it!" he yelled.

"It was the magic lamp!" said
Katy. "It granted your wish!"

"There's no such thing as a
magic lamp," tutted Charlie.

Just then, Pat arrived at the farm.

"Watch me, Pat," called Tom. "I can skateboard!"

"He made a wish on the magic lamp," said Katy.

"Why don't you have a go, Pat?" suggested Tom.

"Well, I . . . er . . . all right then!"

Pat zoomed across the yard . . . WHEEE! . . .

. . . and leapt over a stone, driving Jess into the flower trough!

"MRREOW!"

"Oops, sorry, Jess!" giggled Pat. " I think I'd best be getting on!"

Tom and Katy went to help their mother pick plums in the orchard. As Julia filled the basket, she lost her balance and fell off the ladder.

"Mum! Are you all right?" cried Katy.

"I think I've sprained my ankle," groaned Julia.

Tom ran to fetch Pat.

"We'd better call Dr Gilbertson," said Pat, when he arrived.

He helped Julia hobble into the house.

Dr Gilbertson gently bandaged Julia's ankle. "You need to rest it for a day or two," she said.

"Oh dear!" groaned Julia, "now the wasps will get my plums!"

"Can't we pick them for you?" asked Katy.

"No, I'm afraid not," said Julia. "Going up ladders is for grown-ups."

"I know," said Katy, "let's make a wish on the magic lamp. Let's wish that all the plums are picked!"

"I don't believe in magic," frowned Charlie.

"Well if we make another wish, we'll find out if the lamp's magic or not," said Tom. "Come on!"

They ran off to the mill.

Ted was still up his ladder, painting.

"What shall we wish for?" asked Katy.

"Something fun!" laughed Tom, rubbing the lamp. "We wish something funny would happen!"

The next minute, Ted came down the ladder, and put his foot right in to the paint bucket! "Oh 'eck!" he grumbled.

The children tried to get the bucket off Ted's foot.

"One, two, three . . . PULL!"

Suddenly the bucket flew off . . .

. . . and landed on Ted's head!

"Oh no! We're sorry, Ted," gasped Katy. "We didn't mean THAT to happen!"

"I wish Pat was here," muttered Tom.

And suddenly, he was! Pat was looking for Jess.

"Gosh!" gulped Charlie, "it DOES work!"

Tom quickly rubbed the lamp.

"I wish the bucket would come off Ted's head!"

"You've used all the wishes up, Tom," Katy sighed.

"I think we'd better ring Dr Gilbertson again!" said Pat.

Dr Gilbertson squeezed
soap inside the bucket.

Then she gently eased
the bucket off Ted's head.

"Oooh, my nose!" he groaned.

"We're sorry, Ted," wailed Tom. "It's all our fault. We found a lamp!"

"It's magic," said Katy. "We made three wishes and they all came true!"

"I didn't think they would, but they did!" added Charlie.

"We could have wished for something really useful," Katy sobbed. "And we wasted them all."

"It's not your fault," smiled Pat. "Lamps don't grant wishes, you have to make them come true yourself. If you had another wish, what would it be?"

"Pick the plums!" said Tom and Katy.

So they all got to work.

"That's three hundred and twenty-three plums!" announced Charlie, tapping on his calculator.

"We're making our wish come true, Mum!" beamed Tom and Katy.

"All it takes is a little effort and a little help from your friends," said Pat.

"Thanks everyone," grinned Julia. "You're so kind."

"No trouble!" said Ted, grabbing hold of a branch to steady himself, and showering poor Jess with plums.

Mieow!

SIMON AND SCHUSTER
First published in 2007 in Great Britain by Simon & Schuster UK Ltd
Africa House, 64-78 Kingsway
London WC2B 6AH
A CBS Company

Postman Pat® © 2007 Woodland Animations, a division of Entertainment Rights PLC
Licensed by Entertainment Rights PLC
Original writer John Cunliffe
From the original television design by Ivor Wood
Royal Mail and Post Office imagery is used by kind permission of Royal Mail Group plc
All rights reserved

Text by Alison Ritchie © 2007 Simon & Schuster UK Ltd

All rights reserved including the right of reproduction in whole or in part in any form

A CIP catalogue record for this book is available from the British Library upon request

ISBN-10: 1-84738-001-8
ISBN-13: 978-1-84738-001-2
Printed in China

1 3 5 7 9 10 8 6 4 2